Enid Blyton's
Second Bedtime Book

BY THE SAME AUTHOR

In this series
Enid Blyton's First Bedtime Book
Enid Blyton's Third Bedtime Book
Enid Blyton's Fourth Bedtime Book

Also available for younger readers
The Boy Who Turned into an Engine
The Book of Naughty Children
A Second Book of Naughty Children
Ten-Minute Tales
Fifteen-Minute Tales
Twenty-Minute Tales
More Twenty-Minute Tales
The Land of Far-Beyond
Billy-Bob Tales
Tales of Betsy May
Eight O'Clock Tales
The Yellow Story Book
The Red Story Book
The Blue Story Book
The Green Story Book
Tricky the Goblin
The Adventures of Binkle and Flip
Mr Pink-Whistle's Party
Merry Mr Meddle
Mr Meddle's Mischief
Don't Be Silly Mr Twiddle
Adventures of the Wishing Chair
More Adventures of the Wishing Chair
Rag Tag and Bobtail
Tales from the Bible

Enid Blyton

Second Bedtime
Book

DRAGON
Granada Publishing

Dragon Books
Granada Publishing Limited
8 Grafton Street, London W1X 3LA

Published by Dragon Books 1984

First published by Arthur Barker Ltd, 1955

Copyright © Darrell Waters Ltd, 1955

ISBN 0 583 30663 2

Printed and bound in Great Britain by
Collins, Glasgow
Set in Times

Contents

HE KNEW THE WAY!

Belinda didn't much like the dog next door. 'He's too barky,' she told her mother. 'And too jumpy. Every time he sees me he comes rushing out round my legs, barking like anything, and he makes me jump.'

'It's only because he's pleased to see you,' said Mummy.

'Well, I'm never pleased to see *him*,' said Belinda. 'I think he's silly and stupid, and I don't like him.'

7

So, whenever she saw Winky the dog, she didn't say a word to him, or even look at him if she could help it. She wanted to make him see that she thought he was a silly little thing. But he couldn't seem to understand, and every time he saw Belinda he tore round her, barking with joy.

Belinda often went to see her Granny, and sometimes Winky tried to come with her, because he dearly loved a walk. Belinda didn't want him to come. She tried to send him back home, and stamped her foot when he wouldn't go. He trotted off at last, with his tail down, when she gave him a smack.

Each Saturday Belinda went to see her Granny all by herself, and came home by herself too. She was very proud of that.

She set out one Saturday with a little cake that Mummy had made for Granny. Just as she got to the gate, Winky appeared as usual, and barked loudly, leaping about all round her.

'Oh, you dreadful dog,' said Belinda. 'Go home, I tell you.'

But Winky had smelt the cake she was carrying and he didn't mean to go home! Belinda shut him in his garden and hurried off quickly. Aha! Winky couldn't come this time!

But he managed to jump over the little garden wall and went scurrying after Belinda. And, just as she reached her Granny's, there was Winky, sniffing behind her, trying to find out where the nice smell of cake came from!

HE TROTTED OFF, WITH HIS TAIL DOWN.

Granny was in bed and very pleased to see Belinda. 'I'm not very well to-day,' she said. 'Sit and read to me a bit, dear. Oh, what a lovely cake! We must each have a slice of it.'

Belinda stayed for some time, reading. Then Granny said she must go. So she kissed her Granny, put on her coat, and went to the front door.

And when she got outside, what a shock!

It had suddenly got foggy, and Belinda could hardly see across the pavement. She took a step or two and felt rather frightened.

BELINDA STAYED FOR SOME TIME, READING.

She went out of the front gate and turned down the road.

When she came to a corner, she stopped. She couldn't see where to go! Everything looked so different in the fog. She couldn't see any houses she knew, she didn't know which way to go.

'I'm lost,' said Belinda, in alarm. 'Lost in the fog! There's nobody about. I might wander all night long and never find my way home!'

Suddenly she felt something touching her hand. She jumped and looked down. She saw

Winky! He must have sat outside Granny's and waited for her to come out.

'Oh, Winky,' she said, 'I've never liked you, but I'm really very glad to see you now. Are you lost in the fog too? Don't leave me, will you? We'll be company for one another.'

She was so afraid of Winky leaving her that she felt in her pocket for some string she kept there. She took it out, unrolled it, and tied one end to Winky's collar. He didn't seem to mind. He licked her hand all the time.

Then he began to trot away, and pulled at the string. Belinda had to go with him,

He licked her hand all the time.

because he wouldn't stop. On and on they went, across roads and round corners. Belinda was almost crying.

'We're getting more and more lost,' she told Winky. 'Do, do stop!'

He stopped and pawed at a gate. Belinda peered down at it. It had a name on. 'UPTON LODGE.'

'Good gracious! That's where you live, Winky, next door to us!' cried Belinda joyfully. 'You've come all the way home in the fog – and you've brought me too, because I live next door! I think you're very, very clever.'

She let him go, and ran to the next gate. That was her own, of course, and she was soon safely indoors.

When the fog cleared on Monday Belinda went out and bought a ball. Who for? Yes, for Winky, of course.

'You *must* have a reward for taking me home in the fog,' she said. But the nicest reward he had, of course, was being friends with Belinda. He really did love that!

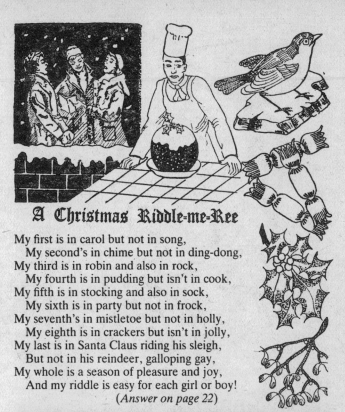

A Christmas Riddle-me-Ree

My first is in carol but not in song,
  My second's in chime but not in ding-dong,
My third is in robin and also in rock,
  My fourth is in pudding but isn't in cook,
My fifth is in stocking and also in sock,
  My sixth is in party but not in frock,
My seventh's in mistletoe but not in holly,
  My eighth is in crackers but isn't in jolly,
My last is in Santa Claus riding his sleigh,
  But not in his reindeer, galloping gay,
My whole is a season of pleasure and joy,
  And my riddle is easy for each girl or boy!
(*Answer on page 22*)

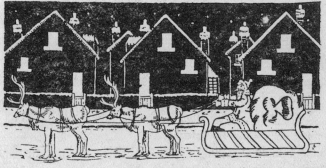

13

WHERE'S MY BICYCLE?

Billy had a very nice bicycle – but, dear me, how careless he was with it! He was always leaving it about and forgetting where he had left it. Once he even came home without it, and had to go all the way back to his Auntie's to fetch it.

His father was cross with him. 'Look here, Billy,' he said, 'that bicycle of yours cost a lot of money. One of these days you'll have it stolen, the way you leave it about. Look, here is a padlock, Now, when you leave your bicycle anywhere, outside a shop, perhaps, or outside a friend's house, slip this chain and padlock on the back wheel, and lock it, then no one can go off with your bicycle.'

'Oh, bother!' said Billy. 'What a nuisance to have to keep doing that, Daddy!'

'Very well. If it's such a nuisance, don't have your bicycle,' said Daddy, in a voice that Billy didn't like at all. 'I'll sell it.'

Billy looked at his father in alarm. He was the kind of father who meant what he said, and Billy half thought he might go and get the bicycle out of the shed then and there, and go off to sell it!

'No, Daddy – no, don't do that,' said Billy. 'I don't want to have to walk to school – and not be able to join the boys on their bike-rides.'

'Well, it's up to you, then,' said his father. 'Either you take care of your bicycle as I have said, and prevent it from being stolen – or you go without it.'

'I'll take care of it,' promised Billy. 'I really will.'

'Well, you'll get a spanking if you don't,' said his father. 'I'm tired of telling you to take care of your things. I work hard and earn money to buy you things like bicycles and roller skates and trains – and you treat them as if you could get them at two a penny. It won't do.'

BILLY WAS VERY CAREFUL AFTER THAT.

Billy was very careful after that. For some time he padlocked his bicycle whenever he left it anywhere. And then, as you can guess, he lost the key to the padlock!

'Bother! Now Daddy will be cross with me for being careless again,' thought Billy. 'I suppose I ought to go and tell him I've lost the key, and he'd get me another. Well, I'll wait a bit, just in case the key turns up.'

He looked for the key, but he couldn't find it. He asked Rita, his sister, if she had seen it, but she hadn't. 'Golly, you *will* get into a row if you don't find it,' she said. 'You'll be leaving your bike somewhere, unpadlocked, and somebody will steal it – and then Daddy will go up in smoke!'

16

After a bit Billy forgot about the lost key. He forgot about having promised to padlock his bicycle. He just went back to his old ways and began to leave his bicycle, here, there and everywhere!

And then he got a dreadful shock!

He had gone to buy a new football with Jack. Jack had no bicycle, so Billy wheeled his along, whilst Jack walked. He was forbidden to take him on the back wheel, of course, because that was dangerous.

They went to the toyshop, but it had no footballs. So they went along to the sports shop, and there they bought a most magnificent ball!

'I say! Isn't it a beauty?' said Jack, bouncing it as they came out of the shop. 'What about going on to the green and having a kick?'

Well, Billy didn't think about his bicycle at all. He had left it outside the toyshop, and hadn't even wheeled it along to the sports shop when they had gone there – and now here he was kicking the new football on the green, not even knowing if his bicycle was still safe outside the toyshop or not! He really was a careless boy.

The two of them had a good game, and then Jack said he must go home. Billy walked off with him, still forgetting about his bicycle.

But Jack remembered it. 'I say – didn't you have a bike?' he said suddenly. 'You were wheeling one when we went to the toyshop. Where did you put it?'

THEY BOUGHT A MOST MAGNIFICENT BALL!

'Gracious! That's where I left it – outside the toyshop!' said Billy. 'Goodness, I hope it's still there.'

'You ought to padlock it,' said Jack. 'My uncle always padlocks his since he had one stolen.'

They went back to the toyshop – and will you believe it, the bicycle had gone! It simply wasn't there. Billy and Jack looked all round and about for it, they went into the shop and asked about it, but it was no good. Nobody knew anything about it at all!

'It's been stolen,' said Jack. 'Bad luck, Billy. What will your father say?'

'I'll get a spanking, I know that,' said Billy, gloomily. 'And I shan't get another bike. I'm scared of going home and telling Dad.'

But he had to go home, of course. He made up his mind to go and tell his father at once. He'd get it over then. He thought about the lost padlock key. Why hadn't he owned up about a little thing – now he had to go and own up about a much bigger thing!

THE BICYCLE HAD GONE!

His father was writing in his study. Billy knocked and went in. 'What is it?' said his father. 'Oh, you want your Saturday money, I suppose?'

'Er, no – it's not that,' said Billy, going as red as a beetroot. 'Dad, I've got something awful to confess.'

'What is it?' said his father at once, looking at him.

'Dad, my bicycle has been stolen,' said Billy not daring to look at his father.

'What – chain, padlock and all!' said his father.

'DAD, I'VE GOT SOMETHING AWFUL TO CONFESS.'

'No,' said Billy, in a low voice. 'Just the bike, Dad. I didn't put the padlock on.'

'Why not?' said his father, sternly.

'Because I lost the key,' said Billy. 'Ages ago that was. I should have come to tell you. Now my bike's gone from outside the toyshop.'

'You deserve a spanking for this,' said his father. 'After all the warnings I gave you, Billy! I'm disappointed in you and ashamed of you. I'm afraid you'll have to be spanked to make you remember this.'

'I'll remember it because my bike's gone,' said poor Billy, in a trembling voice. 'I'm awfully sorry, Dad. I know I deserve to be punished. It was a lovely bike.'

Just then he saw a very surprising sight indeed out of his father's study window. He saw *his bicycle* being ridden up and down the garden path by his sister Rita. HIS BICYCLE! Billy couldn't believe his eyes. He stood and blinked – but it was true. Rita was on his bicycle.

He rushed to the window and opened it. 'Rita! Where did you find my bicycle?'

'Outside the toyshop!' called back Rita. 'I saw it there and you weren't anywhere about at all – so I guessed you'd forgotten it and I rode it home for you.'

Billy sat down in a chair very suddenly. He felt so relieved and thankful that he couldn't say a word. He looked at his father.

'A real let-off for you,' said his father. 'In

RITA WAS ON HIS BICYCLE.

another two minutes you'd have been getting a spanking. I'm not sure you don't deserve one, anyway. What do you say?'

'Yes – I do,' said Billy. 'But if you let me off, Dad, I'll never be such an idiot again. Never! I really did have a terrible shock!'

So he was forgiven and since then nobody could have taken more care of his bicycle than Billy – he cleans and polishes it until it shines like silver. There isn't one *speck* of rust on it – his father is very pleased and proud of Billy now. Still, I shouldn't like to be in his shoes if he's careless again, would you?

ANSWER TO RIDDLE-ME-REE.
Christmas

Sarah's Spelling

'Have you any homework to do, Sarah?' asked Mummy after tea.

'Yes – horrible old spelling!' said Sarah with a groan. 'Look at this list. I've got to learn all these words for to-morrow. I think it's a shame. I do so want to read my new book.'

'Well, dear, learn your spelling first,' said Mummy. 'I know what you're like when you begin a book – you have to read it to the end! Then you'll rush your spelling and not know a single word!'

Mummy went out of the room. Sarah looked at her new book – an adventure story. It did look so exciting. She read the first page

– yes, it was going to be good. She must, she simply MUST read it straight away.

But there was her spelling. She knew she wouldn't bother about it if she didn't learn it now. Sarah gave a tremendous sigh and took up her spelling list. She began to spell the words over and over again.

'R-a-i-n-b-o-w, Rainbow. M-o-o-n-l-i-g-h-t, Moonlight. D-e-w-d-r-o-p, Dewdrop. T-o-a-d-s-t-o-o-l, Toadstool.'

It took her just five minutes to learn them, because she was so determined to be quick – and then, just as she was going to pick up her book, Mummy called her.

'Sarah! Do run to the farm and ask for our eggs, will you, dear? I quite forgot about them to-day.'

'Bother!' said Sarah to herself. 'I did want to read. All right Mummy,' she called. 'I'll rush there and back.'

She took a basket and raced off. She got the eggs and began to run back. 'I'll take the short cut through the wood,' she thought. So she made her way through the trees – and quite suddenly she stopped.

She saw a surprising sight. Three little men were solemnly chalking a white ring in a clear space between the trees. Their beards reached the ground!

'Brownies!' thought Sarah in delight. 'I often wondered if there were any in this quiet little wood! What are they doing?'

She crept behind a tree and watched. One

SHE SAW A SURPRISING SIGHT.

of the brownies stood up and spoke to the others.

'Now all we want for our spell is a small rainbow, a tiny bit of moonlight, one shivery dewdrop and a new-grown toadstool. Once we've got those, we can make our spell.'

'And how do we get them?' asked another little man.

'We all step into this ring and sing the magic words we know – and then we spell RAIN-BOW and a little rainbow will come – and we spell all the other things we want and they'll come, too. So we can take what we need and make our spell!'

Sarah watched, excited. How very, very queer – all the things they wanted had been in her spelling list that day! The three brownies stepped solemnly into the ring and took hands. They danced round, singing words so magic that Sarah shivered. Then they stopped.

'Toadstool first,' said one. 'Now then, all

THEY DANCED ROUND SINGING MAGIC WORDS.

together. T-o-a-d-s-t-o-o-l, TOADSTOOL COME!'

And to Sarah's amazement a brand new toadstool grew in the middle of the ring. One of the brownies picked it. 'Now dewdrop,' he said.

'D-e-w-d-r-o-p, DEWDROP COME!' chanted the three, and suddenly a shining dewdrop appeared at the top of the little hood one of the brownies wore. It quivered there, glittering brightly.

'Now moonlight,' said the little man, and they all solemnly chanted again, 'M-o-o-n-l-i-g-h-t, MOONLIGHT COME!'

A shaft of silvery moonlight lay suddenly across the ring. One of the brownies took a pair of scissors and snipped a piece out. He put it into his pocket. 'Now rainbow,' he said. They all opened their mouths to chant, and then they stopped.

'How do you spell it?' said one. 'R-e-i-n-b-o-w?'

'Yes,' said the others, so they all stood and chanted it. 'R-e-i-n-b-o-w, RAINBOW COME!' But, of course, it *didn't* come. The little men stared round the ring, looking worried.

'Something's gone wrong,' said one. 'We didn't spell it right. Bother! How is it spelt?'

Sarah simply couldn't help coming out from behind her tree. '*I* know how to spell it,' she said. 'It was in my spelling list to-day. It's r-a-i-n-b-o-w.'

SARAH SIMPLY COULDN'T HELP COMING OUT FROM BEHIND
HER TREE.

'Thanks very much,' said the brownies, and
they opened their mouths and chanted. 'R-a-i-
n-b-o-w, RAINBOW COME!'

And a tiny little rainbow shimmered round
them in the ring! One of the men rolled it up
and put it carefully into his pocket. 'Thanks
very much, little girl,' he said. 'You just came
in time.'

'What spell are you making? asked Sarah,
anxiously.

28

'A spell to make a doll come alive,' said the little fellow. 'Good-bye and thank you again.' They all went off and Sarah skipped home, her eyes shining.

'I know the spell to make my doll come alive!' she thought. 'Well, who would have thought my spelling would make a spell? Do all spells have spelling in them? I suppose they do. That must be why they're called spells!'

And to-night she's going to use the spell herself. I hope she spells everything right – it would be such fun to have a doll come alive!

Track him down!

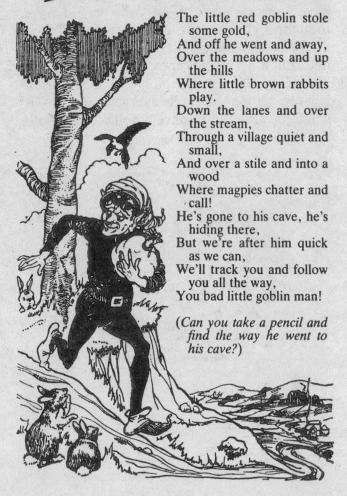

The little red goblin stole
   some gold,
And off he went and away,
Over the meadows and up
   the hills
Where little brown rabbits
   play.
Down the lanes and over
   the stream,
Through a village quiet and
   small,
And over a stile and into a
   wood
Where magpies chatter and
   call!
He's gone to his cave, he's
   hiding there,
But we're after him quick
   as we can,
We'll track you and follow
   you all the way,
You bad little goblin man!

*(Can you take a pencil and
find the way he went to
his cave?)*

They didn't believe in SANTA CLAUS

'Now, is everything ready?' called Santa Claus, as he sat in his sleigh on Christmas Eve, holding the reins of his four reindeer. 'Is my sack quite full? Have I got my notebook with the children's names and addresses in?'

'Yes. You've got everything, sir,' said his servant. 'Better go now, or you'll be late. The reindeer have just had a good meal and they'll be able to gallop well.'

So off went Santa Claus through the night! The reindeer galloped through the frosty air, high above the towns and villages, their bells jingling as they went. 'I've lost count of how many times I've been out like this on Christmas Eve now,' said Santa Claus to himself. 'Is it one thousand or eleven hundred – or even more? I just can't remember.'

He leaned down and looked at the town he was passing over. 'Dear me, the things they have now that they didn't have in years gone by!' he said. 'Aeroplanes, for instance – and those funny H-shaped things on the roofs of some of the houses – what do they call them – television aerials!'

The reindeer galloped on, high above the roofs. Santa Claus looked at his list. He pulled at the reins as they came to a village. 'First call here,' he said. 'Let's see now – Gladys Hills and Sheila Pratt, Bobby and Jean MacDonald. All good children who deserve to have their stockings full from top to toe.'

The reindeer landed gently on the roof of a house, just by a chimney. In a trice Santa Claus had disappeared down the chimney. One of the reindeer put his nose down to see where he had gone. The soot made him sneeze. He was a young one, pulling the sleigh for the first time that Christmas.

They soon left that village and went to another, and then on to a town. And here the accident happened.

A Princess had come to visit the town the day before, and a tall flag-mast had been put up, with a flag right at the top. The flag still flew there, flapping in the wind.

Now the young, new reindeer didn't know what a flag was, and when he saw this flapping thing high up in the air, he was terrified. He reared up and almost upset the sleigh.

'Now, now!' cried Santa crossly. 'Behave

SANTA CLAUS FELL OUT.

yourself, there!'

But the flag flapped again, and that was too much for the reindeer. He reared again, and then pulled away to the left, galloping with all his might, dragging the other three with him.

Alas! When the sleigh tipped up for the second time, Santa Claus fell out. His sack didn't though. Somehow or other that stayed safely on the sleigh. The reindeer disappeared into the night leaving Santa Claus on the roof of a cottage. He hadn't had far to fall, luckily. He sat there, getting his breath.

'Here's a thing to happen!' he said crossly. He wondered what to do. He felt for his whistle to whistle his reindeer back, but that had fallen off somewhere.

'Well, I must get down the chimney and ask for help,' thought Santa, and down the chimney he went.

It was a long chimney and landed him in a cold, empty, dark room. He stepped out on to a hearthrug and at that very moment somebody switched on a light.

An old man stood at the door, and behind stood a fierce-looking old woman. The man held a poker and he came into the room holding it as if he was going to hit Santa Claus.

'Hey, don't do that,' said Santa, in alarm. 'Don't you know me? I'm Santa Claus.'

THE MAN HELD A POKER.

The old man snorted rudely. 'What will you burglars think of next?' he said. 'Dressing up like that and coming down chimneys! *I* know what you've come for – to steal our silver.'

'Look here – I really am Santa Claus,' said Santa. 'Don't you believe me?'

'No. As if we believe in Santa Claus at our age!' said the old woman. 'In fact – I don't believe I *ever* did!'

'Oh, you naughty story-teller,' said Santa. 'Just let me remember now – weren't you once a little girl called Sarah Jane? And didn't I bring you a doll with black hair, blue eyes and a dress with pink roses all over it?'

'My name *is* Sarah Jane,' said the old woman, looking surprised. 'And, yes – I do remember the doll. But *you* didn't bring it – my mother must have given it to me.'

'And isn't this your brother?' went on Santa. 'Let me see – as far as I remember he wasn't a very nice little boy. His name was Peter John – and I brought him a toy boat called *Lucy-Ann*, and a book called *Eyes and No-Eyes*. Yes, I remember that clearly. Years and years ago it was.'

The old man lowered the poker and stared in surprise. 'I don't know how you know all this,' he said. 'It's true my name is Peter John and I did have those things when I was a small boy – but it's no good trying to deceive *me*! You're no more Santa Claus than I am! You're a burglar wearing a silly disguise! And what's more I'm going to call the police!'

'YOU'RE NO MORE SANTA CLAUS THAN I AM!'

'Do,' said Santa Claus, sitting down in a chair. 'I shall probably know the policeman too. Do hurry up, though. I simply *must* get my reindeer back, and time's getting short. I've lots to do to-night.'

'Go and telephone, Sarah Jane,' said the old man to his sister, and she went into the hall. It wasn't long before a knocking came at the door, and two policemen walked in, one middle-aged and plump, the other young and shy.

'Arrest this fellow,' said the old man. 'He broke into my house and came down the chimney dressed up as Santa Claus. Pretends to know all about us – the fraud!'

Santa Claus got up and held out his hand to the plump, middle-aged policeman. 'Why, if it

37

'WHY, IF IT ISN'T HARRY JONES,' HE SAID.

isn't Harry Jones,' he said. 'Harry, you were one of the top children on my list forty years ago – best boy in the village, and I was to bring you a railway train with a tunnel and signal. I did, too – with a station thrown in because I was pleased to hear about you!'

The burly policeman gaped. His eyes almost fell out of his head. 'Sir,' he said, 'sir! My, I haven't believed in you for years! Oh, that railway set! I never had such a wonderful Christmas in my life as I had when I got that railway. I wrote you a letter of thanks, sir.'

'I got it,' said Santa Claus. 'Nicely written, too. And I know this young fellow here as well – why, it can't be more than twelve years ago since I took him a fishing rod and a set of garden tools!'

'Seventeen years, sir,' said the young policeman, grinning all over his face. 'Nicest present I ever had, sir. I made my garden look lovely with those tools. I've still got the fork, sir.'

'You know, I had a letter this Christmas from a small boy called Bobby Brown,' said Santa Claus, fishing in his enormous pocket. 'You're called Bobby Brown, too, aren't you? Any relation?'

'Yes, sir. He's my little boy,' said the big Bobby Brown, blushing red with delight. 'What did he ask you for, sir?'

'An aeroplane and a box of chalks,' said Santa Claus, reading the letter. 'I had them in my sack for him, too. Now, goodness knows if I'll be able to fill any stockings to-night, with my reindeer gone off in a fright!'

The old man was listening to all this in a fine rage. He rapped the poker on the table. 'Police, do your duty. Surely *you* aren't taken in by this fellow. *You* don't believe in Santa Claus, do you?'

'Well – I didn't till I met him – not since I was a kid,' said Bobby Brown. 'But how can I help knowing it *is* Santa Claus, sir? He did bring us those things when we were children. We can't arrest him. We can only help him.'

'Fine, fine,' said Santa. 'Have you got a police-whistle on you? I've dropped my reindeer whistle – but I daresay yours would do as well.'

'Here, sir,' said the young policeman

THE FIVE WATCHERS SAW A SHADOW IN THE EASTERN
SKY.

eagerly, and he handed Santa Claus his whistle. Santa went to the window, opened it and blew three long blasts on the whistle and seven short ones. And in no time at all the five watchers saw a shadow in the eastern sky and heard the sounds of bells. The four reindeer landed on the roof and waited for their master.

He disappeared up the chimney. 'Thank you,' he said to the policemen. 'So glad you still believe in me. Sarah Jane and Peter John don't, though, poor things!'

They didn't! Even though they had seen

and heard him, they still didn't believe it was Santa Claus. What a pity!

Little Bobby Brown got his aeroplane and his chalks – and, will you believe it, the two policemen each got a little present, too – a tiny figure of Santa Claus to put on top of their Christmas cakes. They *were* pleased!

I hope nothing happens to Santa Claus this Christmas – but if it does and he comes into *your* house, help him, won't you! He really is the jolliest, kindest old fellow anyone can meet.

I've got a bone!

A POEM BY MY DOG

I've got a bone,
A glorious bone!
And *where* shall I hide my bone?
If I hide it anywhere near the cat
She'll smell it out in a trice – that's flat
Oh, where shall I hide my bone?

Oh my bone,
My glorious bone,
My nibbley, bitey smelly old bone!
If I bury it down in the garden bed
The gardener will find it and eat it instead,
Oh, *where* shall I hide my bone?

I'll *eat* my bone,
My glorious bone,
That's how I'll hide my bone!
No one will find it – it won't be there,
And the cat can snuffle around, and stare
She won't find my precious bone!

THE FRIENDLY OLD TOAD

'Oh! Here's a horrible toad!' said John, and he lifted his foot to stamp on him. But his father looked at him so sternly that he stopped.

'I shall never take you out with me again if you act cruelly,' said his father. 'Never. Why do you call him a horrible toad? Look at him – he's ugly, sure enough, but see his beautiful eyes!'

John looked at them. Yes, certainly the toad had lovely eyes. 'Like copper,' said John. 'But, Daddy, I thought toads were horrid creatures.'

'Well, don't think it any more,' said his father. 'The toad is a good friend to us. He's a slow old thing but he's clever in his own way. Watch what he does when I bend down to him.'

He bent down suddenly. The toad, afraid, seemed to freeze into the earth. He looked just like a clod, the same colour, and he was very difficult to see.

'That's one of his tricks when an enemy comes by,' said Daddy. 'He "freezes" to the earth. And he has another trick too – a most unpleasant one for any enemy.'

'What's that?' asked John, looking down at

'WATCH HIM CATCH HIS DINNER.'

the old brown toad. 'Does he jump away like a frog does? That's a very clever trick, I think, because it startles any enemy, and gets the frog away quickly.'

'The toad can't do that,' said Daddy. 'His legs aren't long enough. He can only crawl, or do little hops. No – his trick is to pour out an evil-tasting juice all over his back! Then, if his enemy tries to bite him, he finds that the toad tastes so horrible he won't go near him again!'

'Clever old toad,' said John. 'Has he any other tricks, Daddy?'

'Oh yes. Watch him catch his dinner,' said Daddy. 'Look – here comes a blue-bottle fly!'

The blue-bottle buzzed round the toad. He suddenly opened his mouth, shot out a long tongue, drew it in again, blinked and swallowed – and the fly was gone!

'Quick work!' said John. 'What a marvellous tongue he's got, Daddy!'

'Yes – it's fixed to the front of his mouth instead of to the back as yours is,' said his father. 'So he can fling it out a long way. It's sticky at the top, too, and he catches scores of flies in quite a short while.'

'Shall we put him into the ditch?' asked John.

'No,' said Daddy. 'We'll take him home and put him into the garden. He'll be a very good friend there. He'll catch flies and slugs and caterpillars of all kinds. We shall have better salads and vegetables if we make him our friend.'

So they carried him home and called him Crawler the Toad. He still lives in John's garden, and I see him there whenever I go to tea. It's much better to make a toad into a good friend than to kill him, isn't it? You should see how Crawler loves to feel John tickling his back with a bit of grass!

TWO LITTLE PUZZLES FOR YOU

I am a creature in a little round house. Take off my head and I will grow on your fingers. Change my head and you will see me from the station platform. Now add yet another head and I am something left by my first!

(*Answers on page 58*)

Sit down in me and take your ease
Behead me – (brush me nicely, please)
Behead me once again and lo
You breathe me everywhere I go!

Find the three words!

(*Answers on page 66*)

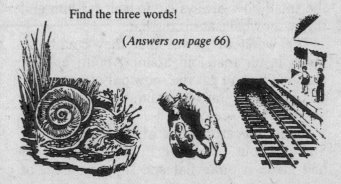

MR STAMP-ABOUT LOSES HIS TEMPER

Mr STAMP-ABOUT didn't like the snow. For one thing, it made him walk slowly, and he didn't like that, because he liked to stamp about in a hurry. And for another thing the small boys always lay in wait for him and threw snowballs at his big hat.

The worst of it was that they could run much faster than old Stamp-About, and by the time he had got the snow out of his collar, and picked up his hat again, there was never anyone to be seen!

'Wait till I catch you! Just wait!' stormed Mr Stamp-About, stamping in the snow till he had made it quite flat and slippery. But, of

48

course, nobody ever did wait to be caught by Mr Stamp-About.

'The little wretches never knock off Mr Twiddle's hat,' he said. 'It's always mine! I'm always the one people play tricks on, and I don't like it. The very next time I'll complain to Mr Plod the policeman. Yes, I will.'

So he did. A well-aimed snowball not only knocked off his hat, but the snow spread itself all over his face too, and he couldn't see anything for a minute or two. You can guess how he roared and stamped about! And off he went to Mr Plod at the police-station.

'I've been snowballed again!' he shouted at Mr Plod. 'My hat's a wreck! I've icy snow-water all down my neck! Why don't you catch the little pests who do this to me? What's a policeman for, I'd like to know?'

'Now, now, Mr Stamp-About,' said Mr Plod. 'No need to shout at me. *I'm* not the one who played tricks on you. And how can I catch anyone if I don't know who they are? You don't even know their names to tell me.'

'How can I know them?' roared Stamp-About. 'They hide till I come – and then I'm so blinded by snow I can't see them.'

'If you could just *catch* one of them,' said Mr Plod, and Mr Stamp-About almost blew him over with his scornful snort.

'Pooh! *Catch* one! They're as slippery as eels. Aha – if ever I do I'll tie him up properly, and bring him to you, Mr Plod. And I hope you'll put him in prison.'

'WHAT'S A POLICEMAN FOR, I'D LIKE TO KNOW?'

'Well, you bring him to me and I'll see,' said
Mr Plod. 'Now, I've no more time to listen to
you this morning, Mr Stamp-About, so don't
begin all over again.'

Mr Stamp-About wasn't used to being
spoken to like this, and he went purple in the
face. But he couldn't say another word
because Mr Plod picked up the telephone
receiver and began to have a very important
conversation with the Inspector. Mr Stamp-
About really didn't dare to interrupt. So he
went out, muttering angrily. If only he could
catch somebody playing a trick on him!

Now, that evening Mr Stamp-About had to
go and see his old friend, Mr Loud-Voice,
who was ill with a cold, and was very upset

because he had lost his voice. Mr Stamp-About stamped about his room, talking loudly, and poor Mr Loud-Voice was quite glad when at last he went.

It was when he was going home that things began to happen to Mr Stamp-About. He was walking along by Dame Old-One's house when suddenly something struck him.

It was snow! It struck Mr Stamp-About on the head, and quite knocked him over! He fell to the ground and the snow trickled down his neck in the horrible cold way it has.

Mr Stamp-About was so angry that he could hardly get up. What a snowball! Why, it must have been the very biggest one that had ever been thrown at him! He had almost been

ONCE MORE HE SANK DOWN UNDER A MASS OF SNOW!

51

buried beneath it! Now where was his hat? That was buried in the snow, too.

Mr Stamp-About was looking for his hat when he was struck by something again – and once more he sank down under a mass of snow! He struggled up, and glared all round. Who was this, throwing enormous snowballs at him in the night? WHO WAS IT? If only he could see them!

Aha! What was that? A figure hiding over there, at the corner? There was nobody else in sight. That was the wicked snowball-thrower! He thought Mr Stamp-About couldn't see him in the darkness, did he?

Mr Stamp-About didn't bother about his hat. Let it stay in the snow! He crept over the road, and then suddenly threw himself on the waiting figure, with a very fierce cry indeed. 'Got you! Got you at last!'

Down went his victim into the snow, his face buried in it so that he could only gasp and splutter. He began to struggle. He was big and strong, which did not surprise Mr Stamp-About at all. Anyone able to throw such enormous snowballs must certainly be very strong!

But Stamp-About was bigger and stronger. He soon managed to tie up arms and ankles with his tie and his belt. Then, because the fellow was heavy, he dumped him back in the snow and tied up his mouth with his handkerchief so that he couldn't call for help.

'And now,' said Mr Stamp-About to the

'GOT YOU AT LAST!'

struggling, trussed-up fellow, 'I'm off to the police station to get Mr Plod – and you'll soon find yourself spending the night in prison! Aha! I'll teach you to go about throwing snowballs at a person like *me*!'

Off he went. He soon arrived at the police-station and shouted for Mr Plod. Mr Plod's assistant looked out of his room.

'Mr Plod's out on his rounds,' he said. 'Anything I can do?'

'I want you to come and arrest a fellow who's been lying in wait for me, and threw such enormous snowballs at me that I was completely buried under them,' said Mr Stamp-About fiercely.

'Oh, I'll have to wait until Mr Plod comes back,' said the assistant. 'Can't leave the police-station with nobody in it, you know. Where's this fellow?'

'Tied up at the corner,' said Stamp-About. 'You come along and take him to prison.'

'I tell you we must wait till Mr Plod comes back,' said the assistant. 'Anyway, if the fellow is all tied up he can wait. Do him good.'

So, very impatient indeed, Mr Stamp-About sat down and waited for Mr Plod. But Mr Plod didn't come. 'Must be on a case,' said the assistant. 'Burglary or something. Don't worry about the prisoner you've left out in the snow. I tell you it'll do him good to think about things a bit.'

'MUST BE ON A CASE,' SAID THE ASSISTANT.

'I dare say – but I want to get home to bed,' snapped Mr Stamp-About. 'It's cold in here. I'm getting tired of waiting.'

But still Mr Plod didn't come. And then at last, just as the police-station clock was striking midnight, Mr Stamp-About heard voices.

'There's Mr Plod!' said the assistant, pleased. 'But doesn't he sound angry. I wonder what's happened.'

Mr Plod stalked into the police-station, red with anger and shivering with cold. With him were two villagers, Old Man Wise and Father Wait-A-Bit.

'Sorry I'm so late,' he said to his gaping assistant. 'Some idiot leapt on me in the dark, got my face down in the snow and tied me up so that I couldn't shout or move! Wait till I get him. Just wait!'

'If I hadn't heard him muttering behind the hanky that was tied across his mouth he wouldn't have been found till morning,' said Old Man Wise.

'We just managed to untie him before he fainted with the cold,' said Father Wait-A-Bit. 'What a shocking thing it is that anyone should dare to attack and tie up our own policeman. The fellow must be caught!'

'And sent to prison for five years,' said Old Man Wise.

'No, twenty years!' raged Mr Plod, trying to get warm by the fire.

Now Mr Stamp-About had been listening to all this in great surprise and horror. What – it

55

'Twenty years!' raged Mr Plod, trying to get warm by the fire.

was MR PLOD he had tied up – the police-man himself! Good gracious! What a truly terrible thing to do!

Mr Stamp-About began to edge out of the room. The assistant saw him. 'Oh, wait a minute – you wanted to ask about . . .'

But Stamp-About no longer wanted to ask anyone anything. All he wanted was to get home to bed and hope that Mr Plod wouldn't hear anything about his waiting there all even-ing for him to arrest somebody that he, Stamp-About, had pounced on and tied up in the snow!

He went back home as quickly as he could. He suddenly remembered his hat. Where was it? Oh yes, he had left it buried in the snow by Dame Old-One's house! He had better go and get it.

He was fumbling in the snow there when suddenly he was struck down again. Whoooosh! Snow covered Stamp-About from head to foot! He sat down in a hurry, buried in snow.

What! Was there *still* someone about waiting to throw snowballs at him? No, it couldn't be. It must be – yes, it *must* be snow sliding off Dame Old-One's roof! It wasn't someone throwing enormous snowballs at him after all!

Whoooooooo . . . began the snow on the roof again, and Stamp-About just skipped

HE DIDN'T GO TO SLEEP ALL NIGHT.

aside in time before another fall of snow crashed down. The snow everywhere was melting and here and there it was sliding off the steeper roofs, falling into gardens and on to pavements.

'I've been an idiot,' said Mr Stamp-About, as he hurried home. 'I thought a roof-fall was a snowball – I pounced on Mr Plod thinking he was the one who had thrown the snow at me – and goodness knows what he'll do to me to-morrow when he hears all I've done. Prison for twenty years, he said. Well, I shouldn't be surprised!'

Poor Mr Stamp-About. He didn't go to sleep all night – and now it's morning and he's waiting to hear the footsteps of the policeman come plod-plod-plodding down the street. Well, well – unpleasant things always happen when people stamp about and lose their tempers!

ANSWERS TO PUZZLE.
Snail, Nail, Rail, Trail.

Draw this picture yourself

You may think it is very difficult to draw an elephant, but it isn't if you do it this way!

Take a pencil and put the point on to dot No. 1. Now look for No. 2 and draw a line up to it. Now on to No. 3, then to No. 4, and so on. Yes, you're drawing an elephant, aren't you! When you have come to No. 56, which is the last number, you will find that you have a fine elephant on this page.

THEY RAN AWAY

'L ET'S run away!' said Bill. 'I'm fed up with the farm.'

'So am I,' said Ben. 'Who'd live on a farm if they could live in a town?'

'Cinemas every night!' said Bill.

'Buses, trains, lots of people, everywhere noise and lights and something going on. How exciting!' said Ben.

'Nothing ever goes on at a farm,' said Bill. 'It's a dead-and-alive place. Nothing to do. No one to talk to. Nowhere to go. Come on – let's go now!'

So they went, that bright spring morning. They caught the bus, and they came to the big town in two hours' time. It was grand! The noise, the traffic, the shops, the people. My, this was life!

They went for rides on buses. They went walking in the crowded streets, and were pushed here and there. They went to two cinemas, and then found that they were so tired they could do nothing else but go to bed. They found a woman who let them have a hot, stuffy, smelly little room for the night.

But they couldn't go to sleep.

'I do miss my dog, Rusty,' said Bill. 'He'll be wondering where I am.'

'And my dog Scamp will be howling for me,' said Ben.

'I reckon old Buttercup and Daisy, the cows we milk, will wonder where we are,' said Bill.

'And Captain and Blossom, the horses – do you suppose they're all right?' said Ben.

'Those little lambs we've fed with the bottle,' said Bill. 'I keep on thinking of them. Growing into frisky little things they are.'

'I hope Pa's shut the hens in all right,' said Ben. 'That fox is about again, you know. I shouldn't want him to get those little chicks.'

'Or the ducklings either,' said Bill.

'I guess that field of corn's going to come along well this weather,' said Ben.

'What do we care about that?' said Bill. 'We won't be there to see it. We'll be here.'

They lay still for a few minutes. Then Ben suddenly threw off the covers. 'I want my dog Scamp,' he said. 'I shouldn't have left him behind.'

'Well, I want my dog Rusty, too,' said Bill. 'Come on – we'll go back and get them.'

UP RAN THREE WELL-GROWN LAMBS.

So back they went, walking mile after mile in the moonlight. At last they came to the farm. They stood at the gate of the Long Field.

'Corn's grown a bit to-day, I do declare,' said Ben.

A bleating came to their ears and up ran three well-grown lambs. They butted their heads against the boys' legs. 'Why, it's our bottle-fed lambs!' said Bill. 'Frisky, Scamper and Wriggle.'

'Moo-oo!' said a voice, and Buttercup, the cow, looked over the hedge. Daisy looked over, too. Ben reached up and rubbed their noses. 'Are you glad to see us back? My, you should just see the big town, Buttercup!'

There was a thudding of big hooves. That was Captain, the great shire horse. He neighed. Ben got up on the gate nearby and hugged the big brown head to him.

'Captain! Who groomed you to-night? Did you miss me?' asked Ben. 'Hallo, Blossom. Bill, here's Blossom looking for you.'

The boys fondled the horses and then went quietly through the moonlit farmyard. They peeped into the hen-house, they looked at the ducklings cuddled with their foster-mothers in a coop or two. They stroked Ribby, the stable cat, and asked how her kittens were.

THERE WAS A THUDDING OF BIG HOOVES.

And then there came such a barking that they were nearly deafened! It was Rusty and Scamp locked up in the stables nearby. They scraped excitedly at the door, and went quite mad with joy at hearing their young masters' voices again.

Ben opened the door. The two dogs flung themselves on them, whining and yelping. They licked every bit of bare skin they could find, hands, knees, faces, necks, ears.

'Oh, Rusty! I'll never leave you behind again!' said Bill.

'And I'm going to take Scamp wherever I

THE TWO DOGS FLUNG THEMSELVES ON THEM, WHINING
AND YELPING.

go!' said Ben, hugging his dog. 'How *could* I have gone without him?'

'Better start back again,' said Bill, after a bit. 'Have to be gone before Pa gets up in the morning.'

'I'm tired,' said Ben. 'I guess I'll go and have a bit of a snooze in the barn before I start back.'

'So will I,' said Bill. 'Come on, Rusty – you can cuddle up to me.'

In two minutes all four were sound asleep, and they didn't wake till the sun was streaming in through the door of the barn.

'My word – there's Buttercup mooing,' said Bill sleepily. 'She wants to be milked. I'll do the cows this morning, Ben – you see to the hens, and bring the horses in if Pa wants them.'

'Lovely morning!' said Ben. 'Nice and noisy, too, Bill – hear the hens clucking, and the ducks quacking and old Buttercup mooing, and the dogs barking, and the lark up there singing like mad.'

'Yes. Seems to me there're more creatures about here than there are people in a town,' said Bill. 'And lots more to do – and sunshine and wind to do it in. Reckon I'd rather be too busy down in the country, Ben, than not have much to do in a town.'

'Better to be like Pa – wear out and not rust out,' said Ben. 'Well – what about this running away, Bill?'

'What running away?' said Bill. 'Well – I've

run away to town – and now I've run back to the country – and I just feel I don't want to do any more running away for a very long time.'

'Funny. I feel the same,' said Ben. 'Hey, Scamp, come along – there's work to do down here on the farm. Hey, Pa! You let those horses be! They're *my* job!'

The Wish I'd Wish

If a fairy came to me
And said, 'Now choose what you will be,
Will you be clever, rich or strong?'
I wouldn't keep her waiting long.

I'd say, 'Well, if you wouldn't mind,
I think I'd rather just be kind,
For one who's kind is happy too,
And makes friends all his life-time through.
No bird is fearful of his voice,
He makes each dog he meets rejoice,
And everyone is full of glee
When Mister Kindheart comes to tea!'

It wouldn't matter then if I
Were ugly, stupid, poor or shy,
For nobody would ever mind,
They'd say – 'We like him, he's so kind!'

THE WAY THINGS GO

'Mummy, I'm going to buy you a brooch, with M on, for your birthday,' said Mary Ann, skipping beside her mother as they went down the garden to pick flowers.

'Oh, Mary Ann – how lovely!' said her mother. 'It will be my very favourite brooch, and I shall always wear it. But how will you get the money? You've hardly any.'

'Well, it's really a secret,' said Mary Ann. 'But I'll tell *you*. I've got some little lettuce plants set out in a row, Mummy – twelve of them. And Auntie Hilda says when they are big enough to eat she will give me tuppence each for them. That will be two shillings – and that's what the brooch costs!'

'What a good idea!' said Mummy.

'Yes, isn't it,' said Mary Ann. 'I planted each lettuce myself, Mummy, when it was very *tiny* – the gardener gave me them out of his throw-aways. He said he had too many. And I weeded them and watered them. They are growing beautifully.'

They passed by the tennis court, and suddenly Mary Ann gave a cry. 'Mummy, look! What's this caught in the bottom of the tennis net?'

'It's a poor little hedgehog!' said Mummy, and she bent down to look. 'They sometimes run into the net at night, try to get free and get tangled up all the more. This one is so tangled that I'll have to cut the net round him to set him free, I'm afraid.'

So, with her flower scissors, she cut away the net, and soon the prickly little hedgehog was free. He lay curled up in a tight ball for some minutes and then he suddenly uncurled himself and ran off like clockwork.

'Mummy, can we give him something to eat?' said Mary Ann. 'He's sweet, I love his little snout and bright eyes.'

'We'll give him bread and milk,' said Mummy. 'All hedgehogs love that. Go and ask Jane for some.'

Jane gave Mary Ann a saucer of bread and milk, and Mary Ann carried it carefully out into the garden. She set it down near the

SHE CUT AWAY THE NET.

hedgehog. He curled up into a ball again, frightened.

'Leave him for a while,' said Mummy. 'He'll soon smell the bread and milk and will go to it.'

So they left him quite alone – and in two minutes he had uncurled himself again and was running to the bread and milk. He rested his front paws on the saucer and it tipped a little. He began to lap the milk.

Whiskers, Mary Ann's black cat, came strolling up, wondering what the hedgehog was. It at once curled itself up again.

'It's all right,' said Whiskers. 'I won't hurt you. Anyway I couldn't if I tried, because you're all prickly! I don't want to hurt myself on *you*!'

The hedgehog uncurled and looked at the big cat. 'Have some of my bread and milk,' he said. 'There's plenty.'

'Well, thanks, I will,' said Whiskers, and he began to lap, too. They finished the bowl between them. Then Whiskers sat washing himself as he always did after a meal.

'That was a kind little girl,' said the hedgehog, watching Whiskers. 'I wish I could do something for her.'

'Yes, she's very kind,' said Whiskers. 'So is

THE HEDGEHOG UNCURLED AND LOOKED AT THE BIG CAT.

71

her mother. I don't know how you can help Mary Ann, I'm sure. What can you do?'

'Well, I can catch beetles and slugs and grubs,' said the hedgehog. 'And I know where some very nice toadstools are.'

'The toadstools wouldn't be any use,' said Whiskers, 'but if you can *really* catch slugs, then you could certainly do Mary Ann a good turn!'

'How?' asked the hedgehog at once.

'Well, you know, Mary Ann is growing twelve lettuces in a row, to sell to her aunt,' said Whiskers. 'And I know something she *doesn't* know – there are seven fat slugs waiting to come along and eat up those little lettuces night after night! They've already begun on three of them. In a night or two they'll all be eaten – not one lettuce will be left.'

'I'll catch every single one of those slugs!' said the hedgehog. 'They'll make me a fine supper. What a good way of paying back Mary Ann for her kindness. It's a pity she won't know.'

He followed Whiskers to where the lettuces grew. The slugs were nowhere to be seen, because they were hiding in little holes. But the hedgehog didn't mind waiting. He curled up till night came, sleeping soundly while he waited.

And at night those seven fat slugs came crawling out of their holes. They went to the lettuces, and they began to eat the tender

THEY BEGAN TO EAT THE TENDER GREEN LEAVES.

green leaves.

Then snap – snap – snap – the hedgehog
came along and snapped up one, two, three
slugs. Then snap – snap – snap – that was
another three – and SNAP! That was the
biggest slug of all disappearing down the
hedgehog's throat.

No other slugs came to eat the lettuces. The
rain came and swelled them up. The sun came
and warmed them. They put out more and
more leaves and grew bigger and bigger hearts
each day. Really, they were the finest lettuces
you could see!

And one day Whiskers saw Mary Ann
cutting one to sell. That was tuppence. The

THE NEXT DAY SHE CUT SIX.

next day she cut two. That was fourpence. The next day she cut six because Auntie Hilda was having a party. That was a whole shilling. And the next day she cut the last three, and that was sixpence.

'I've got a two-shilling piece now, Whiskers,' said Mary Ann. 'And that will buy the brooch for Mummy's birthday tomorrow!'

So it did. Mary Ann brought it home in a little box, and wrote a loving birthday message on it. Her mother was *so* pleased to wear it on her birthday!

It's funny the way things go, isn't it? It all began with a hedgehog caught in a net, and ended up with a mother wearing a brooch with

74

M on it – a brooch she will keep all her life long.

Whiskers and the hedgehog had a lot to do with it – but Mary Ann and her mother will never know that – unless you tell them, of course.

My Aeroplane

When I grow up I think I'll buy
   An aeroplane that I can fly;
I'll swing the big propeller round
   And taxi slowly on the ground.
Then in the air I'll rise and see
   The people staring up at me!
Above the rolling clouds I'll soar
   And make my engine hum and roar.
To France and Spain I'll often fly,
   And round the world maybe I'll try
To travel in my areoplane,
   Yes, round the world and back again!
What fun when all the people cheer
   And cry, 'Oh, look, he's safely here!'
I'll wave my hand and laugh aloud,
   And won't the folk at home be
   PROUD!
    (Can you draw your aeroplane?)

ONE DARK NIGHT

Thomas was a funny boy. He was so scared
of things! He couldn't bear to sing alone
in class. He couldn't bear to take anyone's dog
for a walk in case it ran away. He hated going
upstairs by himself at night, and he always had
to have a night-light in his room, because he
was afraid of the dark.

'I just want to tell you this, Thomas,' said
his father one day. 'I'm not going to force you
to be brave – to jump into the sea, or to climb
a tree, or anything like that. Nobody can
make you brave except yourself. But listen – if
ever you have to be brave for *somebody else's*
sake, then that is the time you simply *must*
have courage!'

'I see, Daddy,' said Thomas. 'You mean –
even though I feel as if I can't jump into the

'I SEE, DADDY,' SAID THOMAS.

swimming-pool quickly, like all the others do
– if I saw somebody fall into the river, for *their*
sake I'd have to jump in straight away and
rescue them.'

'That's just what I mean, Thomas,' said his
father, pleased. 'Please remember that. It's
very, very important. The *real* coward is
always somebody who fails other people.'

Thomas did think about that, but nothing
seemed to happen to other people to make
him try and be brave! He was secretly very
glad. He didn't even *want* to be brave.

Then one night he heard his little sister
Janet crying in her bedroom. He called out to
her. 'Janet – what's the matter?'

'Oh, Thomas – I've left my doll out in the garden,' said Janet. 'And I know it's going to rain. She'll get wet, and she'll get a cold, and she'll be so frightened and lonely out there.'

'She won't,' said Thomas.

'She will,' said Janet. 'I'm going out to get her. Poor Rosebud! She'll be so afraid of the dark.'

'You can't go out in the night all by yourself!' said Thomas, sitting up in bed. 'Don't be silly. You're too little.'

'I don't feel little,' said Janet. 'All the same . . . I wish *you'd* go, Thomas. You're much bigger than me.'

Thomas didn't want to go. The very idea of creeping down the dark garden at night made him shiver. Then he thought of what his father had said.

'The real coward is always someone who fails other people!'

'I ought to go instead of Janet,' he said to himself. 'She's afraid, but she's going. I'm afraid, too – and as it's for Janet, I *must* go! Oh, dear!'

'Janet!' he called. 'Get back into bed. I'll go and get Rosebud. Where is she?'

'Down by the hen-house,' said Janet, getting thankfully back into bed. 'Oh, Thomas – you *are* brave!'

Thomas felt a little better. It was nice to be thought brave, even though he was hating every minute of this night walk! He slipped downstairs and out into the garden.

'I'LL GO AND GET ROSEBUD.'

It was very dark indeed. He bumped into a bush. Something flew round his head – was it a bat? He switched on his torch, but no light came! The battery had gone. This was worse than ever!

He groped his way down the garden in the dark, his heart thumping. He was afraid something might grab him – though there was nothing to grab him at all! He was afraid of hurting himself, he was afraid all the time.

He came to the hen-house and wondered where Rosebud was. He saw a little white patch on the steps of the hen-house and felt for it. It was Rosebud – good!

He picked up the doll and was just going back to the house when he heard voices – low voices, nearby. He stood quite still, scared. Who was about at this time of night?

He stepped into the hedge close by, his heart thumping again. The voices were nearer now, and he could hear very quiet footsteps.

'No one about!' whispered someone. 'This is the place, isn't it? Let's hope the hens don't make too much noise! Got the sack?'

And then Thomas knew what was happening, of course! Someone had come to steal his

IT WAS ROSEBUD – GOOD!

81

mother's hens! The hens across the road had been taken – the hens two houses away had all been stolen the week before – and now the thieves were here to take his own mother's hens – the hens she was so proud of, that laid so well. Why, they each had their own name and would come running when they were called!

Thomas stood there, as still as could be. He didn't think of running away. He just thought of his mother's face if she heard next day that all her precious hens had been stolen in the night. She would be very sad indeed.

THE THIEVES WERE HERE TO TAKE HIS OWN MOTHER'S HENS.

But what could he *do*? There wasn't time to go back to the house and warn his father – the hens would have been taken by then.

And he certainly couldn't fight the men – that would be silly. Thomas simply didn't know *what* to do.

Then he remembered something. He had heard a car stop outside in the lane, just as he had come down the garden to look for Rosebud. That must be the men's car. It was still standing out in the lane – would there be another man in it? Perhaps not. If the car was empty, then – then – Thomas could open the door and take out the key that started the car! Without the ignition key, the car could not be started. And so the men wouldn't be able to get away!

What a wonderful idea! But would it work? Thomas slid to the other side of the bush, and ran quietly down the grass to the garden gate that led into the lane. He wasn't afraid of the dark any more – how queer! He wasn't afraid of bumping into things and hurting himself, either. He just thought of that car, and taking its key.

The car was there, with no lights on at all. Thomas went cautiously to it. There didn't seem to be anyone inside. He quietly opened the door nearest the steering-wheel. He put in his hand and groped over the dash-board. He found the key – and he pulled it out! Now the car could not be started!

His heart was beating fast again, but with

HE QUIETLY OPENED THE DOOR.

excitement and triumph now, not with fear. He went back through the gate, hearing the hens cluck in the house as he did so. The men were even now stuffing the poor things into their sack.

He ran all the way up to the house without stopping. He tore in at the door and raced to the sitting-room where his mother and father were sitting, reading. They were amazed to see Thomas at that time of night, panting and excited.

'Mummy! Daddy! There are men stealing the hens. But they can't get away because I've taken the key of their car. Here it is. Can you telephone the police – because they could easily catch the thieves now!'

His mother simply couldn't believe her ears, and she sat and stared. But in a trice his father was at the telephone. 'Police-station, please. Ah – is that Sergeant Harris? I think we've got the hen-thieves here, Sergeant; at Red-Roof House. My boy's taken the key of their car, so they can't get away. If you come now, you can catch the thieves. Yes – yes – he's really got the key – very smart work on his part!'

HE TORE IN AT THE DOOR AND RACED TO THE SITTING-ROOM.

85

'*Thomas!*' said his mother, amazed. 'Do you really – oh, *Thomas* – I would never have thought you could do such a thing. Daddy – isn't it marvellous! Oh, Thomas, I'm so proud of you.'

It wasn't long before a police-car roared up the lane. Its lights picked out the thieves' car. The two men were in it, desperately feeling in their pockets for the key. They didn't dream that somebody had taken it! The hens were in the seat behind in a sack.

Well, that was the last of those hen-thieves! They were locked up, and couldn't go robbing

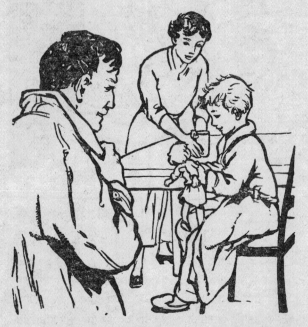

'WHY ARE YOU HOLDING JANET'S DOLL, THOMAS DEAR?'

other people any more. The police were delighted, and they praised Thomas highly.

'He's not only a brave boy, he's a smart one,' they said. 'You should be proud of him, sir.'

'I am,' said Thomas's father, and gave Thomas a very proud smile indeed.

'There's just one thing I'd love to know,' said his mother, when the police had gone. 'Why are you holding Janet's doll, Thomas dear?'

'Oh goodness – I forgot all about it,' said Thomas, and he put Rosebud down. 'You may think I'm awfully brave and all the rest of it, Mummy – but all that happened really was that I went out to find Janet's doll for her. I would have been too scared to go and get anything of my own – but I couldn't let little Janet go by herself.'

'You remembered what I said, old son,' said Daddy. 'No matter how much of a coward you are, you have to be brave if it's for other people.'

'Yes, I did remember that,' said Thomas. 'And when I got down to the hen-house and heard those men, I thought how sad Mummy would be if her hens were stolen, and I didn't feel afraid any more. It's easy to be brave for other people, isn't it?'

'Not so very easy!' said Daddy. 'And now, Thomas, you will find out a very queer thing about yourself.'

'What, Daddy?' asked Thomas.

'You'll find that once having been brave for other people, it's *much* easier to be brave for yourself!' said Daddy. 'You'll see what I mean when you go to the swimming-pool to-morrow. You'll see the cold water, and think "Pooh! If I can tackle hen-thieves in the middle of the night, what's a bit of cold water?" And you'll jump straight in!'

Daddy was perfectly right. Thomas did jump straight in. He knew he could be brave, because he had *been* brave the night before – and so it was easy to be brave again.

Did you know that? It's really worth remembering.

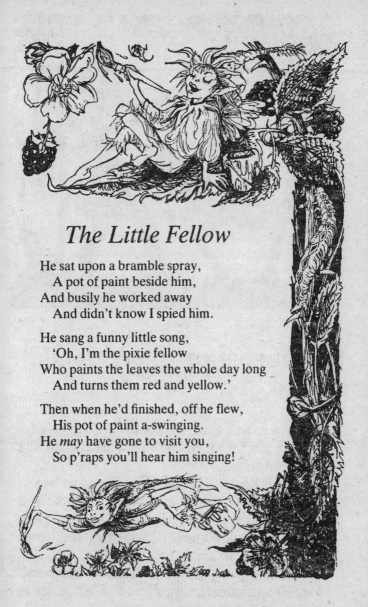

The Little Fellow

He sat upon a bramble spray,
　A pot of paint beside him,
And busily he worked away
　And didn't know I spied him.

He sang a funny little song,
　'Oh, I'm the pixie fellow
Who paints the leaves the whole day long
　And turns them red and yellow.'

Then when he'd finished, off he flew,
　His pot of paint a-swinging.
He *may* have gone to visit you,
　So p'raps you'll hear him singing!

SHE FORGOT TO SAY THANK YOU!

THERE was once a spoilt little girl who always forgot to say thank you when she went out to tea.

We all know that when we say good-bye at the end of a tea-party we must say 'Thank you for having me and for giving me such a lovely time,' and Lucy knew it, too. But she never remembered to say it.

'What a pity Lucy hasn't good manners,' Mrs Brown said. 'Do you know, I asked her to tea yesterday with Ken and Doris, and when she went she never so much as said thank you!'

'And when I took her for a picnic with Tom and Ellen, and paid for her to have a ride on a donkey on the sands, she went home without a word of thanks!' said Mrs Jones. 'Funny, isn't it? Surely all children know they must say thank you when they have been to somebody's tea-party or picnic?'

Aha, but wait! There came a time when Lucy forgot once too often. It happened like this.

She was walking through the wood on her way home from her Granny's when a small man ran round a tree and bumped hard into her.

'Oooh,' said Lucy. 'Do look where you're going. You've broken the egg in this bag. I was taking it home for my breakfast to-morrow. My Granny's hen laid it for me.'

'Dear me! I'm most terribly sorry,' said the brownie. 'Er – I don't know if you've realised it, but I'm a brownie – one of the Little Folk, you know. I must certainly make up to you for breaking your precious egg.'

'How?' asked Lucy, beginning to feel excited.

'Well, would you like to come to a party this afternoon?' said the brownie. 'I'm giving one to six of my friends. It's my birthday, and I'm having a lovely birthday cake with two hundred and thirty-three candles on it.'

'Gracious! Are you as old as that?' said Lucy, astonished.

'That's not very old for a brownie,' said the little man. 'My grandfather is much, much older than that – five hundred and something – I forget exactly. Well, will you come to my party? Three o'clock, and meet me by the big oak tree over there.'

'Oh, yes,' said Lucy, and she ran happily home. She had her dinner by herself because her mother was out. She put on a clean frock at half-past two and did her hair nicely. Then she set out for the big oak tree.

The brownie was there. He took her through the wood to a little clearing. There was a small village there with queer little crooked houses, and the tiniest cats and dogs Lucy had ever seen.

The brownie took her into one of the houses. There were six of his friends there and they all shook hands most politely with Lucy.

On the table was a magnificent birthday cake. You should have seen it! Lucy had never in her life seen such a beauty. 'Well!' she said. 'What a lot of candles! Are there really two hundred and thirty-three? I'd never be able to count them all.'

They looked lovely when they were lighted. The brownie didn't light them with matches but with his wand. He waved it over the cake and every candle lighted at once!

The tea was lovely. There were sixteen different kinds of sandwiches, five different

SHE DID HER HAIR NICELY.

kinds of buns, seven kinds of biscuits and the birthday cake. After that there were rainbow jellies, shimmering with seven colours, and ice-creams that were colder than any Lucy had ever tasted before.

After tea they played all kinds of lovely games. Then there was a bran-tub to dip into, and every guest had a present. Lucy had a tiny musical-box. She loved it.

Then it was time to go. One by one the guests shook hands with the generous little brownie. 'Thank you for having us and for

HE WAVED IT OVER THE CAKE.

giving us such a wonderful time,' they said, very politely. 'It's been lovely!'

Then it was Lucy's turn to say good-bye. She shook hands, and ran down the path. As usual she forgot to say thank you for the lovely time.

But the path led right back to the village! There she was again, outside the brownie's house. He came hopefully to the door, expecting that the little girl had remembered her manners and had come to thank him. But she hadn't!

'Bother!' she said. 'I must have taken the wrong path.'

And off she went again – but in twenty minutes' time she was back in the village once more. How very extraordinary!

The brownie came to the door at once, quite expecting Lucy to say she was sorry for having forgotten to thank him for his lovely party. But she didn't. She just stamped her foot crossly and went off again.

But no matter what path she took she always came back to the brownies' village.

LUCY HAD A TINY MUSICAL-BOX

Soon she began to feel frightened. She called to the brownie.

'What's happening? I can't seem to go home. Every path leads me back here. Why is it?'

'Well – it means you've forgotten something, I think,' said the brownie. 'You see, the paths leading from our village are queer. They always bring people back here if they've forgotten something. They brought my grandfather straight back when he forgot his umbrella.'

SHE ALWAYS CAME BACK TO THE BROWNIES' VILLAGE.

'But I haven't forgotten anything at all,' said Lucy crossly. 'I didn't have a hat – or a bag – or an umbrella.'

'Strange,' said the brownie. 'It's true, you didn't. You haven't left anything behind. What can you have forgotten?'

'I simply don't know,' said Lucy. 'Think hard, brownie. *What* have I forgotten?'

The brownie thought hard. Then he went rather red. 'Well,' he said. 'I hardly like to tell you. It's only a little thing, and it's very queer that the paths keep bringing you back for that. But it's the only thing I can think of.'

'Well, tell me,' said Lucy. 'Why don't you like to tell me? It's not anything dreadful.'

'It *is* something rather dreadful,' said the brownie. 'I feel ashamed to tell you because it will make you feel ashamed, too.'

'OH, DO TELL ME!' cried Lucy, getting impatient.

'It's your *manners* you have forgotten,' said the brownie. 'You forgot to say thank you to me for my party. Everyone else remembered, of course, because they've all been well brought up – but you forgot. Still, perhaps you haven't been well brought up, poor child.'

Now it was Lucy's turn to go bright red. 'I *have* been well brought up,' she said in a small voice. 'I do know I ought to say thank you. I'm very, very sorry I forgot. It was dreadful of me after such a lovely party. Thank you, brownie, for having me and for giving me such a wonderful time.'

'GOOD-BYE, AND I DO HOPE I SHALL SEE YOU AGAIN,'
SAID LUCY.

'That's all right,' said the brownie, looking
pleased. 'I was rather afraid you hadn't
enjoyed yourself when you didn't say thank
you. I'm glad you did.'

'Good-bye, and I do hope I shall see you
again,' said Lucy, trying to be as nice as ever
she could to make up for forgetting her manners. 'I'll bring you a bit of my own birthday
cake when I have it next week.'

She ran off down the path – and will you
believe it, it took her safely all the way home!

So it was quite clear that it was her manners she had forgotten, and that was why the paths kept taking her back to the village.

The week after that Lucy had a birthday party of her own, and the next day she took a piece of her cake to give to the kind little brownie. But it was a pity, she simply *couldn't* remember the way to his village!

Still, there was one thing she always did remember after that – and you know what it was, don't you? Yes – she remembered to say thank you after a party!

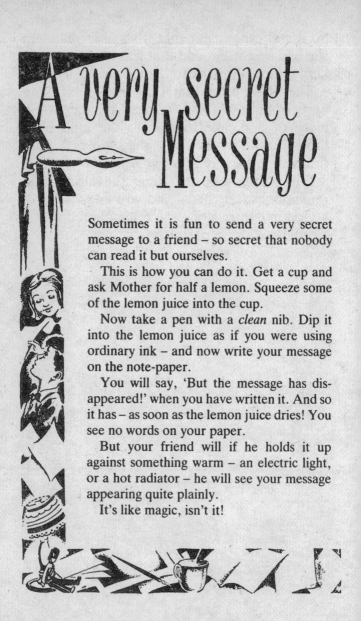

A very secret Message

Sometimes it is fun to send a very secret message to a friend – so secret that nobody can read it but ourselves.

This is how you can do it. Get a cup and ask Mother for half a lemon. Squeeze some of the lemon juice into the cup.

Now take a pen with a *clean* nib. Dip it into the lemon juice as if you were using ordinary ink – and now write your message on the note-paper.

You will say, 'But the message has disappeared!' when you have written it. And so it has – as soon as the lemon juice dries! You see no words on your paper.

But your friend will if he holds it up against something warm – an electric light, or a hot radiator – he will see your message appearing quite plainly.

It's like magic, isn't it!

FOXGLOVE *Fairies*

Some fairies came half-running, half-flying round by the foxgloves in the wood. The foxgloves were much taller than they were, and the fairies stopped to look at them.

'See!' said Winks, bending down to pick up a fallen foxglove bell. 'Wouldn't this do beautifully for a glove-finger! We could sew five together and make some lovely gloves for the little folk, couldn't we? Do let's.'

'The foxgloves might not want us to take their fallen flowers,' said Pippi.

'Well, we'll ask them,' said Chatter. So she called up to the dreaming foxgloves.

'Foxgloves, are you awake? Listen! Can we take your fallen flower-bells to make gloves with?'

'What will you give us in return?' asked the foxgloves.

'What would you like?' said Winks.

'Well, I suppose you couldn't tell us how to stop the tiny insects and small flies from climbing into our bells and stealing our honey, could you?' asked the foxgloves. 'You see, the only visitors we want are the bumble-bees, but so many smaller insects come and steal what we store for the big bumbles.'

'We'll think about it,' said the fairies. So they did, and, of course, they knew what to do at once!

'Can you grow a little mat of hairs at the entrance to your bells?' said Winks. 'That would keep out the tiny flies wouldn't it, for the hairs would seem like a great forest to them!'

'A good idea!' said the foxgloves. 'We will do that. But then the bumble-bees might not see the way up our bells!'

'Well, grow some nice bright coloured spots all the way up to the honey,' said the fairies. 'Then the bees will see them and follow them like a path. We'll tell the bumbles what you put them there for.'

'Thank you!' said the foxgloves, and they grew mats of hair at the entrance of their bells, and put a coloured pathway of spots leading to their honey.

FIRST SHE MEASURED A FOXGLOVE BELL.

'We'll measure you and see if you are the right size to take a bumble-bee's body exactly,' said Winks, and she whipped out her little tape-measure. First she measured a fox-glove bell, and then she measured a fat bumble-bee who was one of her friends.

'Your bells need to be just a tiny bit bigger!' she cried, and the foxgloves nodded in reply.

'Thank you,' they said. 'Now we shall keep our honey safely! The hairs will keep out the smaller insects, the spots will guide the bum-bles, and they will be able to squeeze in nicely, for our bells will be made to fit them! Take as many of the fallen bells as you like, fairies, and make gloves for the little folk from them!'

That's how the foxglove got its name; it is really called folk's glove, not foxglove. Did you know that? And would you like to see the mat of hairs and the pretty pathway of spots put there for the bumble-bees? Well, you go and see!

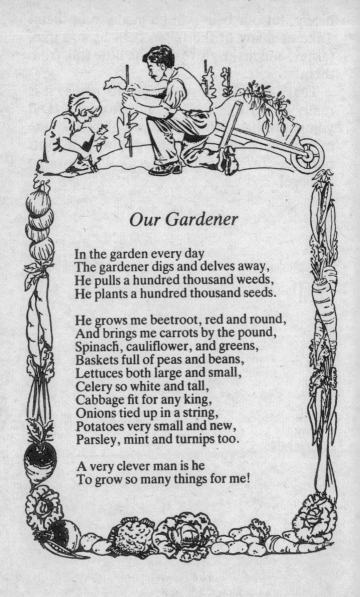

Our Gardener

In the garden every day
The gardener digs and delves away,
He pulls a hundred thousand weeds,
He plants a hundred thousand seeds.

He grows me beetroot, red and round,
And brings me carrots by the pound,
Spinach, cauliflower, and greens,
Baskets full of peas and beans,
Lettuces both large and small,
Celery so white and tall,
Cabbage fit for any king,
Onions tied up in a string,
Potatoes very small and new,
Parsley, mint and turnips too.

A very clever man is he
To grow so many things for me!

THE CHILDREN WHO WEREN'T ASKED

JOHNNIE and Susie Morrison always had a wonderful party just after Christmas. They were twins and their birthdays came then, so their mother put Christmas and birthdays together and gave them a really lovely party!

Johnnie and Susie always enjoyed their party tremendously – but the other children enjoyed it even more! It began at three and lasted till seven, and there was always a fine conjuror and a treasure hunt, too.

Alice and Peter Collins loved the Morrisons' party almost more than anyone else, because they didn't go to many. They thought the Morrisons' party was just as good as Christmas!

'We shall soon get our invitation,' said Alice. 'I know the date – it's the date of the twins' birthday, December 29th. I'm glad I've got a new frock.'

The invitations didn't seem to come as early as they usually did. Christmas came and went, and still no invitation card had come.

'They're leaving it rather late!' said Peter. 'But I know they're having the party as usual, because Mrs Mills, the baker's wife, told me she is making some special chocolate cakes for it.'

'Oooh!' said Alice. 'I can't wait for the day!'

When they went out that morning they saw Joan ahead of them. She called out to a boy across the road. 'Are you going to the Morrisons' party?'

'Rather!' he said. 'I've answered my invitation already.'

Alice and Peter looked at one another, and felt rather sick. So the invitations *had* gone out then! And they hadn't had one.

They went home feeling miserable. 'We've been left out,' said Alice. 'I wonder why?'

'It's funny,' said Peter. 'We've been three times before. Oh, dear – it's so very horrid to be left out, isn't it, Alice? The other children are sure to ask us if we are going.'

'Well, we must just say no, we're sorry we're not,' said Alice.

So when Gladys and Roy and Winnie and Sam met them in the next two or three days, and asked the same question: 'You going to

SHE CALLED OUT, 'ARE YOU GOING TO THE MORRISONS' PARTY?'

the Morrisons' party?' Alice and Peter said what they had planned to say:

'No. We're sorry we're not!'

'It will be awkward if we meet Johnnie or Susie,' said Alice. 'I don't feel as if I like them much now. I hate being left out like this.'

'Well, if we see them we'll cross over or turn down a corner or something,' said Peter. So, whenever they saw the twins in the distance they were careful not to go near them.

Alice worried and worried about it. Had she or Peter done anything the twins didn't like? Did Mrs Morrison think their manners

109

ALICE AND PETER SAID WHAT THEY HAD PLANNED TO
SAY.

weren't good enough? Didn't the twins like
them any more?

Peter wasn't so worried, but he thought it
was mean. Every other child in the village
seemed to be going to the party. It looked
dreadful for them to be left out. Luckily his
mother hadn't seemed to realise it, so that was
all right. It would have worried her, too,
because she was proud of Alice and Peter.

Every morning Alice hoped secretly that
the invitation would come. It might have been
delayed, perhaps. It would turn up, after all!

But it didn't. The day of the party came and
still there was no invitation card. Peter looked
at Alice gloomily.

'It won't be very pleasant seeing all the others going by to the party this afternoon, will it?' he said.

'No,' said Alice, nearly crying. 'And it will be *horrid* at school next week hearing them all talk about it, and we shan't be able to say a word. Oh, I do hate those twins.'

'So do I,' said Peter. 'It's such a mean trick just to leave us two out. Nobody else has been left out at all.'

They went out to the shops for their mother. On the way back they saw a little dog trotting in front of them. It was the twins' cocker spaniel, out on his own.

He ran across the road – and a bicycle came round the corner. It ran straight into the little dog, and the rider almost fell off. He aimed a kick at the frightened dog and rode away.

The dog limped to the kerb. It lay down. It whined pitifully and licked its paws.

'It's hurt,' said Alice. 'Oh, Peter!'

'*Let* it be hurt,' said Peter. 'It's the twins' dog, and it's probably as horrid as they are.'

'Oh, Peter – it's a dear little dog,' said Alice. 'We *must* see to it. We must. You can't be as horrid as you sound!'

Peter wasn't, of course. He was really a very kind-hearted boy, and he went with Alice at once to see to the dog. The dog knew them and whined. Peter picked it up and carried it to his home.

He and Alice bathed the crushed paw and bandaged it. They gave the dog some warm

HE AIMED A KICK AT THE FRIGHTENED DOG AND RODE
AWAY.

milk and fussed it. It licked them and wagged
its tail.

'It's all right now,' said Peter. 'But I don't
know if it can walk. That front paw is really
hurt and this back one looks very sore.'

The dog tried to walk, but it couldn't. It
rolled over and looked helplessly up at the
children, as if to say 'Sorry! But I just can't
walk.'

'We can't possibly carry it to the Morrisons'
door,' said Peter. 'I never want to go into their
gate again! We'll take it to the gate and push it
just inside. Then the Morrisons will find it, or
hear it whining. I just won't speak to that
horrid, unkind family.'

So they took turns in carrying the spaniel to the Morrisons' gate. But Alice was really too kind-hearted to push it inside and leave it. 'I can't,' she said. 'I'll just *have* to take it to the house. I don't care – if I have to speak to those horrid twins – well, it just can't be helped. It's for the dog's sake, after all.'

They marched up to the front door and rang the bell. The door soon opened and there stood Mrs Morrison, smiling at them.

'Oh – has something happened to Scamper?' she said. 'You *are* kind children to bring him back, and you've bandaged his paw, I see. The twins *will* be grateful to you.'

PETER PICKED IT UP AND CARRIED IT TO HIS HOME.

She took the dog and turned to call the twins.

'Come on,' said Peter, in a low voice. 'We don't need to stop now.'

So they went down the path. Mrs Morrison turned and saw them. 'I'll be seeing you this afternoon at the party!' she called. 'I'll thank you properly then, my dears.'

They turned at once. 'But we haven't been *asked*,' said Alice. 'Have you forgotten?'

Mrs Morrison stared in surprise. 'Don't be silly, Alice dear,' she said. 'Of course you and Peter have been asked. Why, your names were among the first to be put down on our list. Do you mean to say you didn't get your invitation?'

'No. We haven't had one,' said Peter.

'Well, how strange!' said Mrs Morrison. 'You *will* come, though, won't you? Why, we've got presents for you and everything! The twins wondered why you hadn't answered. Well, you *must* have thought it queer if you didn't get an invitation like all the others!'

Peter went rather red. Alice looked suddenly excited. 'Can we really come?' she said. 'You *did* mean us to? Oh, Mrs Morrison, how lovely! We did so want to come!'

'NO. WE HAVEN'T HAD ONE,' SAID PETER.

115

'Yes, of course you must come,' said kind Mrs Morrison. 'Three o'clock. And thank you *so* much for looking after our little dog. That just shows what nice children you are, to bring back the dog when you thought we'd left you out!'

The two children rushed off, excited and happy. It was all a mistake! They were to go. They hadn't been left out, after all. What a very good thing they had taken Scamper back to the house!

And now I expect you wonder why they hadn't had an invitation. Well, the twins explained it all that afternoon.

'You see, Mummy put all the invitations into my dolls' pram for me to take to the post,'

THE PARTY WAS TWICE AS GOOD AS USUAL.

said Susie. 'And one slipped under the pillow – yours! We've just found it there. So it wasn't posted. I'm so sorry. But it doesn't matter now you're here.'

No, it didn't matter. Everything was lovely again. Mrs Morrison was kind, the twins were as jolly as ever, and the party was twice as good as usual.

As for the spaniel, he had a new red bow and was made such a fuss of because of his bad leg that he really enjoyed the party more than anyone!

Sally's Sixpence

'SALLY!' called Mummy. 'I want you to go to the newspaper shop for me and fetch me my magazine.'

'Must I?' called back Sally. 'It looks as if it's going to pour with rain, Mummy.'

'Well, take your umbrella, then,' said Mummy. 'I gave you a lovely one for your birthday. You ought to be pleased to use it.'

'Mummy, my shoes let in the wet,' said Sally, trying to think of another excuse not to go.

'Well, put on your rubber boots, then, if your shoes want mending,' said Mother. 'Here's sixpence. Now you go along at once, before the shop shuts. Your umbrella and your rubber boots are in the hall cupboard. Hurry, Sally.'

Sally took the sixpence. Bother! Now she would *have* to go – and she did so badly want to finish her book.

She put on her rubber boots. She put on her coat. She took her umbrella. She held the sixpence in her hand and she set off.

Well, it began to pour with rain, just as Sally had thought it would. How it pelted down!

She put up her umbrella and trotted down the road, hoping there would soon be puddles she could splash through. Mummy didn't mind her going through puddles if she had her boots on.

The rain stopped very suddenly. Sally put down her umbrella. She came to the news-paper shop and walked in.

'Can I have Mummy's magazine, please?' she said. But when she wanted to pay for it the sixpence wasn't in her hand. It was gone.

'Oh, dear – I must have dropped it,' said Sally, and back she went, hunting along the road for the sixpence. But it was quite gone.

She went home, upset. 'I've lost the sixpence, Mummy,' she said. 'I'm so sorry. I didn't hear it drop or I would have known I'd lost it. I can't imagine *where* it is!'

'That's careless of you, Sally,' said her mother. 'Here's another sixpence. Now don't you dare to come back and say you've lost that one too!'

'Of course not,' said Sally, and she set off again, holding the sixpence tightly in her hand and the umbrella in the other. It wasn't raining any more, so she didn't need to have it up this time.

She splashed through a puddle and made

'CAN I HAVE MUMMY'S MAGAZINE, PLEASE?' SHE SAID.

SHE SPLASHED THROUGH A PUDDLE.

such a shower of drops that some went down into the rubber boots. 'Oh, dear,' she said, and looked to see if her socks were wet. They didn't seem to be. She walked on to the shop – and will you believe it, when she got there she hadn't got the sixpence again! She stared at her empty hand in dismay.

'Well! Your mother won't be at all pleased with you!' said the shopkeeper, and put the magazine back on the shelf again.

Sally nearly cried. This was most mysterious. *Another* sixpence gone! Well, she must have dropped it by that big puddle she splashed through. That's where it must have gone.

So back she went to the puddle. She looked into it. She looked all round it. She looked in the road and by the side of the road. No sixpence.

'Bother! Somebody must have come by and picked it up,' said poor Sally, and went home very slowly indeed, afraid that Mummy would be crosser than ever.

But she wasn't. She was sorry to see Sally's frightened, upset little face. She patted her.

'Never mind! It was my fault for sending

THEY GOT TO GRANNY'S.

122

you shopping with money. You're too little to take care of it yet.'

'I'm not really,' said Sally, in a small voice. 'I kept them both carefully – and then they just disappeared. I'm sure I didn't drop them. I would have heard them if I had. It must be a magic spell, Mummy.'

'In that case, they'll probably come back again,' said Mummy. 'We'll hope so, anyway! Now keep your rubber boots and coat on, because Granny has just telephoned to say will we go and have dinner with her to-day. We'll go now.'

Well, that was nice. It was always fun to go to Granny's. Sally set off with Mummy, carrying her umbrella in case it rained again. But it didn't.

They got to Granny's She was at the front door, waiting for them. She smiled when she saw them.

'Well, well, here's little Sally with her new umbrella!' she said. 'Let's have a look at it, Sally!'

She took it and opened it – and, dear me, down on the top of Granny's head fell a sixpence. A little silver sixpence. She was most surprised.

'Oh!' squealed Sally. 'There's one of the sixpences, Mummy. It was down the umbrella! Oh, I'm so glad!'

'Well, now perhaps the other will turn up,' said Mummy, laughing. 'Come along, we must go in.'

SHE PULLED ONE BOOT OFF – AND THEN THE OTHER.

'Take off your big boots first, Sally,' said Granny. 'Are they hard to get off? Sit down on the little porch seat and I'll help you.'

She pulled one boot off – and then the other. And out of the second one shot – a little silver sixpence!

'Well, goodness gracious, child, are you *made* of sixpences!' cried Granny, in surprise.

'Mummy! Mummy! The other sixpence was in my boot!' squealed Sally. 'I didn't lose that one either.'

Well, wasn't that peculiar? Sally couldn't help thinking there might be some magic about. One sixpence in her umbrella, and the other in her boot – very queer.

And will you believe it, when she got home she felt in her pocket – and there was a silver sixpence there, too! That was very extraordinary, because Sally knew she had only had her hanky there when she set out to Granny's.

'There *is* magic about,' she said happily. 'So you can't blame me for losing sixpences any more, Mummy. I can't help it if there's magic about.'

But I shouldn't be surprised if Granny had popped that sixpence in her pocket for a surprise, would you? It's the sort of things Grannies do – the nice ones, anyway!

THE END

Books by **Enid Blyton** for young readers

All these books are available at your local bookshop or newsagent, or can be ordered direct from the publisher.

To order direct from the publisher just tick the titles you want and fill in the form below.

Name_____

Address _____

Send to:
Dragon Cash Sales
PO Box 11, Falmouth, Cornwall TR10 9EN.

Please enclose remittance to the value of the cover price plus:

UK 45p for the first book, 20p for the second book plus 14p per copy for each additional book ordered to a maximum charge of £1.63.

BFPO and Eire 45p for the first book, 20p for the second book plus 14p per copy for the next 7 books, thereafter 8p per book.

Overseas 75p for the first book and 21p for each additional book.

Granada Publishing reserve the right to show new retail prices on covers, which may differ from those previously advertised in the text or elsewhere.